And the Cow Said Moo!

BY **MILDRED PHILLIPS**

PICTURES BY **SONJA LAMUT**

 Greenwillow Books

An Imprint of HarperCollinsPublishers

Egg tempera and oil paints were used for the full-color art.
The text type is Kabel Demi BT.
And the Cow Said Moo!
Text copyright © 2000 by Mildred Phillips
Illustrations copyright © 2000 by Sonja Lamut
Printed in Singapore by Tien Wah Press. All rights reserved.
http://harperchildrens.com

Library of Congress Cataloging-in-Publication Data

Phillips, Mildred.
And the cow said moo! /
by Mildred Phillips ;
pictures by Sonja Lamut.
p.   cm.
"Greenwillow Books."
Summary: A cow questions why the other animals
make their own sounds, instead of saying, "MOO!" as she does.
ISBN 0-688-16802-7 (trade).   ISBN 0-688-16803-5 (lib. bdg.)
[1. Animal sounds—Fiction.   2. Cows—Fiction.
3. Domestic animals—Fiction.   4. Identity—Fiction.]
I. Lamut, Sonja, ill.   II. Title.
PZ7.P546An   2000   [E]—dc21   99-14356   CIP

1 2 3 4 5 6 7 8 9 10 First Edition

For Meaghan, Ally,
& Madison B.
—M. P.

For my daughter, Anna
—S. L.

"Good morning, Sheep.
Say Moo! Say Moo!
If I say Moo, why don't you?"

"We **Ba-a-a**," said the sheep.
"That's what sheep do.
Ba-a-a!" said the sheep.
And the cow said, "**Moo!**"

Along came Duck.

"Good morning, Duck.
Say **Moo!** Say **Moo!**
If I say **Moo**, why don't you?"

"We **Quack!**" said the duck.
"That's what ducks do.
"**Quack-Quack!**" said the duck.
"**Ba-a-a**," said the sheep.
And the cow said, "**Moo!**"

Along came Dog.

"Good morning, Dog.
Say **Moo!** Say **Moo!**
If I say **Moo**, why don't you?"

"We Woof!" said the dog.
"That's what dogs do.
Woof-Woof!" said the dog.
"Quack-Quack!" said the duck.
"Ba-a-a!" said the sheep.
And the cow said, "Moo!"

Along came Pig.

"Good morning, Pig.
Say **Moo!** Say **Moo!**
If I say **Moo**, why don't you?"

Oink Oink Oink   Oink Oink   Oink Oink Oink Oink Oink Oink Oink Oink

"We Oink!" said the pig.
"That's what pigs do.
Oink-Oink!" said the pig.
"Woof-Woof!" said the dog.
"Quack-Quack!" said the duck.
"Ba-a-a!" said the sheep.
And the cow said, "Moo!"

Along came Horse.

"Good morning, Horse.
Say **Moo!** Say **Moo!**
If I say **Moo**, why don't you?"

"We **Neigh!**" said the horse.
"That's what horses do.
Neigh!" said the horse.
"**Oink-Oink!**" said the pig.
"**Woof-Woof!**" said the dog.
"**Quack-Quack!**" said the duck.
"**Ba-a-a!**" said the sheep.
And the cow said, "**Moo!**"

Along came Owl.

"Good morning, Owl.
Say **Moo!** Say **Moo!**
If I say **Moo**, why don't you?"

"We **Whoooo**," said the owl.
"That's what owls do."

"Now if I said **Moo**,
and you said **Whoooo**,
you'd be me
and I'd be you!"

"I'm me!" said the cow.
"I'm a cow. I **Moo**.
I'm glad I am me
and I'm glad you are you."

"**Neigh!**" said the horse.
"**Oink-Oink!**" said the pig.
"**Woof-Woof!**" said the dog.
"**Quack-Quack!**" said the duck.
"**Ba-a-a!**" said the sheep.
The owl said, "**Whoooo**," . . .

and the cow said, "Moo!"

Ba-a Moo Quack Woof Moo Quack Whooo Who
Neigh Woof Moo Neigh Woof Whoooo
Oink Moo Ba-a-a Neigh Whoooo Oink Neigh Moo Quack Woof Neigh
Quack Woof Whoooo Oink Whoooo Moo Quack Oink Moo Neigh
Moo Neigh Quack Ba-a-a Woof Oink Moo Ba-a-a Neigh
Oink Woof Whoooo Neigh Neigh Quack Whoooo Woof
Neigh Ba-a Whoooo Oink Moo Neigh Quack Whoooo Oink
ooo Moo Quack Woof Moo Oink Ba-a-a Whoooo Oink
Woof Oink Moo Neigh Woof Moo Woof Who
igh Moo Ba-a Whoooo Oink Ba-a-a Quack Oink
Whoooo Quack Woof Moo Woof Quack Whoooo
Moo Quack Neigh Woof Ba-a-a Neigh Who
Woof Oink Moo Neigh Woof Moo Woof
Ba-a Neigh Neigh Ba-a-a Neigh Woof
Whoooo Oink Whoooo Moo Quack Whoooo Neig
Neigh Quack Ba-a-a Woof Oink Moo Quack
Woof Whoooo Neigh Quack Whoooo
Oink Quack Neigh Ba-a-a Neigh Woof
Moo Whoooo Oink Moo Neigh Quack
Neigh Ba-a Woof Whoooo Oink Who
ooo Moo Quack Neigh Woof Moo Woof Wh
gh Oink Moo Quack Ba-a Whoooo Oink